Airplanes have made traveling fast and easy

AN *Airport*

Melissa Gish

A⁺

Smart Apple Media

COPYRIGHT

Published by Smart Apple Media

1980 Lookout Drive, North Mankato, MN 56003

Designed by Rita Marshall

Printed in the United States of America

Photographs by Corbis, Image Finders (Jim Baron), Sally Myers,
Tom Stack & Associates (Gary Milburn, Charles Palek, Brian Parker, Bob Pool,
Tom & Therisa Stack, TSADO/NASA)

Library of Congress Cataloging-in-Publication Data

Gish, Melissa. An airport / by Melissa Gish.

p. cm. — (Field trips) Includes bibliographical references and index.

Summary: Briefly describes what goes on at an airport, some of the people who
work there, and the job of controlling traffic in the air. Includes a related activity.

ISBN 1-58340-322-1

1. Airports—Juvenile literature. [1. Airports. 2. Air traffic control].

I. Title. II. Field trips (Smart Apple Media) (Mankato, Minn.).

TL725.15.G57 2003   387.7'36—dc21   2002042788

First Edition 9 8 7 6 5 4 3 2 1

CONTENTS

AN *Airport*

At the Airport   6

Running the Airport   12

Air Traffic Control   16

Up! Up! And Away!   18

Hands On: Understanding Air Power   22

Additional Information   24

At the Airport

People travel for many reasons. Some travel for work. Some travel for vacation. They may travel across town, across North America, or across the world. Many people who travel long distances do so on airplanes. Airplanes may be small, or they may be very big. The big airplanes, called jet planes, fly in and out of large airports. There are many different things happening in an airport. When people go to the airport, they may need to park their car. People arriving on an airplane

Jet planes pull up to an airport to be boarded

may need a car to use while in a new town. Airports have parking garages where people can park or pay money to borrow cars. ⌘ The part of the airport that is most visible to visitors is the **terminal**. This is where people buy tickets, turn in their **baggage**, and wait to get on airplanes. Airports stay open 24 hours a day because people need to travel all the time. Most terminals are very busy during the day. They may appear quiet late at night,

Many airports pay people to scare birds away from runways because birds can damage airplanes if they fly into engines.

Many terminals have restaurants and shops

Planes need long runways to take off and land

when fewer people travel. But the airport is always active in

ways travelers cannot see.

Running the Airport

It takes many people with different skills to run an airport.

They work hard to provide safety and **security** for people

traveling by air. When people travel on airplanes, they need to

have tickets. Each airplane can hold only a certain number of

passengers. Ticket agents work behind ticket counters in the

airport terminal. The ticket agents sell tickets and keep track of

exactly who is traveling on every airplane that leaves the

airport. ᡣᢩ Most travelers have baggage. They may carry

small items on the airplane with them. Large suitcases or

clothing bags must be "checked." A tag is put on each piece of

Airport workers collect and load baggage

baggage showing its owner's name. Then a worker called a

baggage handler takes the baggage away and stores it in the

bottom, or belly, of the airplane. People may have pets that

need to travel with them. Pets cannot sit **A baggage**

handler uses a

with their owners on the airplane. Pets must **machine that**

can sort about

travel in special crates with the baggage. **500 pieces of**

baggage per

Being safe while traveling on an **minute.**

airplane is important. Security agents are airport workers who

are responsible for airport safety. Security agents must check

all the baggage to make sure it contains only harmless items.

They also check every person getting on an airplane in order

to make sure that nothing dangerous is being carried onto

the airplane.

Security agents use metal detectors and x-rays

Air Traffic Control

Outside the airport terminal is a maze of runways.

Runways are long roads. Airplanes take off and land on the

runways. Airplanes come and go on these **The Boeing**

747-400 is one

roads day and night. All of the **traffic** must **of the world's**

biggest

be carefully managed. This is the job of the **airplanes. It**

can hold 566

air traffic controllers. The air traffic **passengers.**

control tower has glass windows all around it. Controllers have

a clear view of all airplanes on the runways. To watch airplanes

Air traffic controllers keep watch on the planes

that are still in the air, controllers study **radar** screens. **Pilots**

can talk to air traffic controllers on two-way radios.

When an airplane is ready to land at the airport, an air traffic

controller uses a computer to direct the pilot to the center of

the runway and guide the airplane down safely. Air traffic

controllers are especially important at night or in rain, snow, or

fog, when pilots cannot see the ground.

Up! Up! And Away!

The speed of air travel is one reason so many people

like to fly. A boat trip from New York to England could take

six days, but an airplane ride takes just six hours. Millions of

people travel by air each year. At a large airport, thousands of

airplanes fly in and out every day. People come and go to cities

With radar, planes can be seen from far away

around the world. Airports are being designed today to make air travel even more convenient for people. The Denver International Airport in Colorado is one example. It is twice the size of Manhattan Island, and its runways make up 900 miles (1,448 km) of roads. Underground trains carry passengers around the airport.

Two of the busiest airports in North America are Chicago's O'Hare Airport and the Lester B. Pearson Airport in Toronto.

Totally designed, constructed, and managed by computers, it represents the airport of the future.

This jet plane is being loaded before takeoff

Understanding Air Power

This simple experiment will show you how air lifts heavy airplanes into the sky.

What You Need

A strip of notebook paper as wide as your hand
Clear adhesive tape
A square electric fan

What You Do

1. Set the fan on a table. Make sure there is nothing in front of it or behind it.
2. Set the paper flat on the table. Line up the edge of the paper with the bottom frame of the fan and securely tape the edge of the paper to the frame of the fan.
3. Move the fan close to the edge of the table so the paper flops over the edge and turn on the fan.

What You See

At first the paper may not move much. But turn the fan on high, and the paper lifts up. This is because the slow-moving air under the strip pushes against the fast-moving air on top of the strip. As the fan blows faster, the strip flies higher, just like the wings of an airplane.